About the Author

Richard grew up in Southern England and as a child enjoyed carefree days of playing in mud and climbing trees and allowing his imagination to grow from the sights and surrounds around him. Richard has always loved stories of kindness and happy ever afters and always ends his own stories with positive thoughts of encouragement and compassion in some shape or form.

Felix Finds His Fortune

Richard Thomas Carey

Felix Finds His Fortune

Nightingale Books

A CIP catalogue record for this title is
available from the British Library.
ISBN 9781838751241

Nightingale Books is an imprint of
Pegasus Elliot MacKenzie Publishers Ltd.
www.pegasuspublishers.com

First Published in 2021

Nightingale Books
Sheraton House Castle Park
Cambridge England

Printed & Bound in Great Britain

Dedication

I would like to dedicate this book to my life partner and soul mate GC, my mother, Susan, and my sister, Ness. All of whom fill my life with love and encouragement.

Once upon a time, in fact, quite some time ago, there lived a kind and humble little field mouse by the name of Felix. His full name was Felix Ferguson Fieldmouse, and he lived all alone in a somewhat bleak and isolated part of the country, in a small cosy nest made entirely of straw, that stood in a dusty old hollow on the edge of a wheat field. Although he was poorer than a church mouse, he was always the first to help anybody in need and would happily give them his last remaining grain. He had nothing to show but the rags on his back but always managed to remain kind and carefree.

One day when Felix was about to grab his supper, he realised that he was down to his last supply of food, and with winter already creeping around the corner, Felix thought that maybe it was time to move on to better quarters. *What do I have to keep me here*, he thought, looking around at his cold, dusty little hollow. *I don't need much, but it would be nice to find somewhere warm and dry.*

That night poor Felix lay in his dusty straw nest cold and restless, wondering where he should go, when suddenly he had a thought. He remembered that he had a distant cousin in London. *Maybe that would be a good place to head*, he thought, *where I would be away from the cold, harsh winter winds that the countryside always throws at me.*

The next morning Felix was up bright and early, and already to set off on his new adventure. He packed his bag with the remains of his food and went on his way.

He had been walking for what seemed like an awfully long time when a jolly farmer, came along the dusty road in a hay cart. The farmer saw Felix and asked him where he was heading.

'I'm on my way to London, to look for a better life,' he replied.

'I am not going to London, but I will be happy to take you as far as I can,' said the farmer.

'Thank you,' said Felix, as he hopped on board, 'you are very kind.'

After some time, they came to a fork in the road, with a signpost in the middle. 'This is where I must drop you,' said the farmer as he came to a halt. 'If you continue along the road, then you will be heading in the right direction.'

'Thank you, for your kindness,' said Felix, as he climbed down from the cart.

After walking for a short distance, Felix noticed that the light was starting to fade. He looked up at the sky only to find some rather angry looking clouds peering down at him. *I must find a place to sleep tonight*, thought Felix, as he came across an old flowerpot lying along the roadside. *This will do just fine*, he thought as he climbed into the pot.

Just as he started to snuggle up for the night, the rains came tumbling down. Unfortunately, this was when poor Felix discovered that there was a crack in the pot, allowing the rain to seep through all night, which prevented him from getting any sleep at all. He lay there cold and wet, and shivered till the morning sun shone through. Letting out a little sneeze, he nibbled on what remained of his food before setting off on the rest of his journey.

After walking for most of the morning, he came across a small town in the country. Almost ready to drop, he rested along the roadside, when a young delivery boy spotted him.

'Hello,' said the boy, noticing how hungry poor Felix looked, 'would you like to join me for some lunch? I don't have much, but I would be more than happy to share with you what I do have.'

'That is very kind of you,' said Felix as the boy handed him a piece of bread and cheese.

'Where are you off to on such a cold day?' asked the boy.

'London.' replied Felix as he nibbled on a piece of cheese.

'London is a very long way from here,' said the boy, 'but if it helps, I can give you a lift to the next hamlet?'

'I would appreciate that very much,' said Felix with a grateful smile.

'Then climb into the basket, and we will be on our way,' said the boy.

In a short time, they arrived at the next hamlet, where the boy said, 'Well, my little friend, this is where I must drop you.'

'Thank you,' said Felix, 'you have been a great help.'

'It was my pleasure,' said the boy, as he rode off on his way.

Felix had been walking for the remainder of the day when he arrived at the outskirts of the next village. The evening sun had disappeared; and the wind howled as it began to hail. Looking around, he spotted a red post-box across the lane so scurried across and climbed inside, where he sheltered for the night.

Felix slept so well that night that when he woke up the next morning, he found that he was inside a postbag with the morning post. As he peeped out from the bag, he realised that he was heading in the wrong direction. Jumping out as fast as he could, he headed straight back towards the village till he came across a milestone, directing him to London.

Having nothing left to eat, Felix continued his long journey until he could walk no more. As the day was drawing to an end, he was feeling quite exhausted, when suddenly, everything went dark.

The next day after a very long sleep, Felix woke up to the sweet chirping tones of a robin redbreast. 'Well, good morning to you,' she sang cheerfully, as she fed him some water.

'Where am I?' asked Felix in a tizzy.

'Don't you worry your sweet little self about that,' said the robin. 'You are safe and warm and welcome to stay here as long as you like.'

As he lay there in the straw, he saw a great big pair of friendly eyes peering down at him.

'This is the scarecrow,' chirped the robin. 'Thank goodness he spotted you last night, or you may never have survived.'

'You had passed out from exhaustion, and with Jack Frost already leaving his mark, it would not have been a good time to be out there,' said the scarecrow.

'I am forever grateful to you both,' replied Felix as he nibbled on some bread that Mrs Redbreast had given him.

'Happy to oblige,' said the scarecrow with a smile on his face. 'Besides, I love having company in my jacket, some even make it their permanent home,' he said, looking over to the robin, 'and you are very welcome to do the same.'

'That is very kind of you,' replied Felix as he climbed out of the scarecrow's jacket, 'but I really must be on my way, as I am heading to London to see my cousin and to make a new life for myself.'

As Felix climbed on to the scarecrow's shoulder, still a little tired from his travels, a rather eccentric but friendly crow flew in and landed on the scarecrow's hat.

'London, London, did I hear someone say London?' he squawked. 'I am flying in that direction and will happily take you as far as I can, if that is any use to you?'

'That would be very much appreciated,' said Felix, 'if it is no trouble?'

'No trouble at all, just climb aboard, and we will be on our way' said the crow, happily.

As Felix climbed onto the crow's back, he said, 'I thought scarecrows were supposed to scare you off.'

Suddenly the robin let out a little chuckle. 'Scare?' she said. 'Our lovely scarecrow could not scare anything if he tried. He even has the word CARE in his name so he is more of a carecrow than a scarecrow and everybody loves him,' she said, as she handed Felix his bag which she had filled with enough food to see him through.

Later that day the crow landed on the banks of a canal. 'This is where I must drop you,' he said, 'but if you walk along the towpath, you will be heading in the right direction.' 'You still have a long way to go, but I wish you well, my friend.'

'Thank you,' said Felix, 'you have certainly made my journey easier.'

'Oh, I enjoyed the company,' screeched the crow as he flew off, wishing Felix luck for the rest of his journey.

Felix had been walking along the canal for some time when the sky began to change colour, and it began to sleet. *Well, I suppose I had better find some shelter for the night*, he thought as he came across an old boot lying along the canal bank. *This will be as good a place to sleep as any*, he thought, climbing into the old boot.

Early the next morning, Felix woke up to the neighing of a horse. He climbed out of the boot to investigate, only to find an old horse-drawn canal barge getting ready to move. It was going to be pulled by an old shire horse and not one to miss an opportunity, he asked the horse where she was heading.

'I am on my way to London to deliver the goods on board,' she said. 'Hop aboard if you need a lift.'

'Thank you,' said Felix, 'that would be very much appreciated.'

'It will take us a few days to reach London with a few stops in between, but I would be very happy for the company,' said the horse, as she started to pull the barge along.

For the next few days, Felix kept the horse company while resting in her hat. As they arrived in London, the sun was setting so Felix was eager to be on his way. After thanking the horse for her kindness, Felix scurried off along the towpath till he arrived at his cousin's house in Whitechapel. Having not seen his cousin since they were pups made Felix feel just a little nervous, but excited at the same time. He took a deep breath, knocked on the door and waited. Suddenly the door opened and standing there was a very well-dressed little mouse by the name of Terrance Tarquin Tittlemouse.

'Hello, Terrance,' said Felix. 'It's me, your cousin from the country. Please may I come in for some food and shelter for the night,' he asked.

'Not dressed in those rags,' replied Terrance, looking poor Felix up and down through his monocle. 'I have friends here tonight, and if they know that we are related I will be a laughingstock,' he said in a rather snooty voice and slammed the door in poor Felix's face.

'Well, I didn't expect that,' said Felix as he scurried off on his way.

After walking for some time, he came upon the river Thames when suddenly there

was a rumble in the air. He looked up at the sky as the thunder crashed, the lightning flashed, and the rain came tumbling down. *Well, if ever I needed a place to shelter it is now*, he thought, as he came across an old bottle washed up along the bank. After squeezing himself through the neck and into the body, Felix felt safe and sheltered for the night.

The next morning, Felix woke from a lovely sleep as the winter sun shone through the bottle. He was just about to climb out when it rolled straight down the bank and into the Thames. *Oh, bother*, he thought as he splashed into the river, *who knows where I will end up now?*

As Felix floated along the river, a flock of hungry seagulls came swarming down at him. They tried to grab poor Felix by sticking their beaks into the bottle, but luckily, it was far too narrow. However, they continued to tap on the bottle in the hope that it would break, but instead found that it was damaging their beaks so decided to give up.

As Felix continued to float along the river, it suddenly changed course, trapping him into a current that swirled him around and around like a spinning top. Poor Felix was feeling quite dizzy when suddenly and without any warning, the bottle crashed straight into a

rock, shattering into a hundred pieces. Lucky for Felix, he had learnt to swim from a very early age allowing him to swim straight to shore.

As he climbed the banks of the Thames, he noticed that he was on the grounds of the Tower of London. The poor raven master was all of a fluster trying to control some wild cats chasing the ravens around the grounds. Always ready to help anyone in need, Felix went up to the raven master to see if he could help.

'What can a little thing like you do?' asked the raven master, as the cats caused even more mayhem.

'I may be small, but I am extremely fast,' said Felix, as he started to distract the cats.

This pleased the raven master very much; you see there is an old legend that says, if the ravens ever leave the grounds of the Tower of London, then the White Tower will fall and crumble along with the British monarchy and its kingdom. The ravens always have their wings clipped, so that they cannot fly away, and this is why the cats were able to chase them around the grounds. 'I can't pay you anything,' said the raven master, 'but I would gladly give you food and shelter for the night.'

'That is all I need,' said Felix as he continued to distract the cats.

Before long, the cats had had enough and disappeared off the grounds so the raven master thanked Felix for his trouble, giving him food and shelter that night.

The next morning Felix was up bright and early, so headed to the city where he came upon an old market. He saw that the fishmonger was having trouble with some stray cats who were trying to steal his fish. Once again, Felix was happy to help and started to distract the cats away from his stall. After a while, the cats all fled, and the fishmonger was grateful.

'I'm afraid I don't have much to offer you but food and shelter for the night,' he said, 'if that is any use.'

'That's all I need,' said Felix, as he rested his legs.

That evening, the fishmonger took Felix home to his cottage, giving him a warm bed and plenty of food for the night.

Early the next morning, Felix went on his way in search of more work till he came upon Covent Garden. There he met a young milkmaid who, like the raven master and the fishmonger, was having trouble with some dirty stray cats hanging around and trying to steal milk from her pails.

'Would you like me to help you?' said Felix to the milkmaid, as he started to distract the cats away from her stall.

'If you could keep them at bay, I would be very happy,' she said, 'but I don't have anything to pay you with, except for bread and as much milk as you like, and you would be more than welcome to shelter in my humble little cottage for the night if you need to.'

'Thank you,' said Felix, 'that would be very much appreciated.'

That night he sat in front of the warm glowing fire with more than enough bread and milk than he could wish for and before long fell into a profound sleep.

The next morning, Felix said goodbye to the milkmaid as she gave him some bread to see him on his way.

Over the next few days, Felix was unable to find any work but managed to find shelter each night in some shape or form. By the third day, he had run out of food altogether and noticed how the days were getting colder as the snow began to fall.

It was Christmas Eve, and as Felix staggered down Regent Street, through the falling snow, he felt fatigued and ready to drop. Suddenly, he came upon a window with the most magical display you could ever imagine. It sparkled and twinkled with passion and excitement and sitting in the centre was the most beautiful doll's house you had ever seen.

The window had been set up already for Christmas and belonged to the most famous toy shop in the world.

What a perfect place for me to shelter for the night, thought Felix, as he peered through the window. After crawling under the door, he went over to the doll's house, opened the door and straight up the stairs, where he found the perfect size bed. He was so exhausted that night that once he climbed into bed, he fell into the deepest sleep ever.

The next morning, Felix woke up to darkness and when he went downstairs to open the front door, he found that it was stuck. What was preventing him from opening the door and why was it so dark? All of a sudden, Felix heard a loud tearing noise when suddenly the light came beaming through the window. The doll's house had been wrapped up for Christmas and when Felix looked up, he found a little girl staring down upon him. Now this was not just any little girl, but the princess at Buckingham Palace and she had been given the doll's house for Christmas.

She could not have been more delighted with her gift, especially when she found Felix staring straight back at her. 'Oh, I have such a wonderful idea,' said the princess with excitement as she disappeared from the room. Before long she returned with a rather large cage in her hand. *Oh no*, thought Felix, *I have not come all this way to end up in a cage*, but just as he was about to make his escape, he saw the prettiest little white mouse he had ever seen. This was the princess's pet mouse, Wilomena, her full name being, Wilomena Winifred Whitemouse.

'You can both live in the doll's house together,' said the princess. It would be far more fun than having dolls living there as they never do anything but sit in the chairs all day and expect everything to be done for them. 'Not only will I dress you in the finest of clothes but will also feed you the finest of cheese.'

And do you know that as soon as Felix and Wilomena clapped eyes on one another, it was love at first sight and from then on, Felix knew all at once, that he had found his fortune. Not a fortune as in money and wealth, but in love, happiness, friendship and kindness that he had been shown throughout his journey, and do you know that from this day on they lived happily ever after?